SHARPEN YOUR SLEUTHING SKILLS WITH GHOSTWRITER AND HIS FRIENDS IN THIS NEW COLLECTION OF SECRET CODES, FUNNY RIDDLES, AMAZING MESSAGES, AND MORE!

What is the Booksnatcher trying to say here?

The WAKE UP Night

What about here?

AAGGEENNTT

Why do pigs make great chefs?

Perhaps you know what cows do on a Saturday night?

You'll need the answers to catch the Booksnatcher.
The clues are inside!

Join the Team!

Do you watch GHOSTWRITER on PBS? Then you know that when you read and write to solve a mystery or unravel a puzzle, you're using the same smarts and skills the Ghostwriter team uses.

We hope you'll join the team and read along to help solve the mysterious and puzzling goings-on in these GHOSTWRITER books!

Ghost writer™

THE BIG BOOK OF KIDS' PUZZLES

by P. C. Russell Ginns
Illustrated by Bill Basso

A
Children's Television Workshop
Book

BANTAM BOOKS/DELL MAGAZINES
NEW YORK • TORONTO • LONDON • SYDNEY • AUCKLAND

THE BIG BOOK OF KIDS' PUZZLES
A Bantam Books / Dell Magazines production November 1992

Cover art by Michael Kozmiuk.
Interior illustrations by Bill Basso and Nicky Zann.
Typography by Movable Type.

ISBN 0-553-37074-X

Published simultaneously in the United States and Canada

Bantam Books are published by Bantam Books, a division of Bantam Doubleday Dell Publishing Group, Inc. Its trademark, consisting of the words "Bantam Books" and the portrayal of a rooster, is Registered in U.S. Patent and Trademark Office and in other countries. Marca Registrada. Bantam Books, 666 Fifth Avenue, New York, New York 10103. Dell Magazines are published by Dell Magazines, a division of Bantam Doubleday Dell Publishing Group, Inc., 245 Park Avenue, New York, New York 10167. Dell is a registered trademark of Bantam Doubleday Dell Publishing Group, Inc. Published 4 times a year. Single copy price $1.25 U.S.A., $1.50 Canada

PRINTED IN THE UNITED STATES OF AMERICA

0 9 8 7 6 5 4 3 2 1

Have you met the Ghostwriter team?

Jamal. Lenni. Alex. Gaby. Tina. These New York kids have a hot secret: They're good friends with a ghost! That's right, a ghost. They call him Ghostwriter, because he only communicates through written words.

Ghostwriter's past is a mystery. He can't remember who he was when he was alive. The team is helping him to find out. In the meantime, though, there are plenty of other mysteries to solve. The latest: Someone's been sneaking through the neighborhood stealing all kinds of books!

Who is the mysterious Booksnatcher, and how will he (or she) finally be caught? Join the team and their secret friend Ghostwriter as they track the Booksnatcher through these perplexing puzzles!

*Extra: There's a bonus puzzle "running" through this book. If you can find it and figure it out, you'll get a message from Ghostwriter.

Greetings, Detectives!

Oh, no! There's been a robbery. Boy, is Gaby mad! All her trivia books have vanished into thin air. And all the thief left behind is this note:

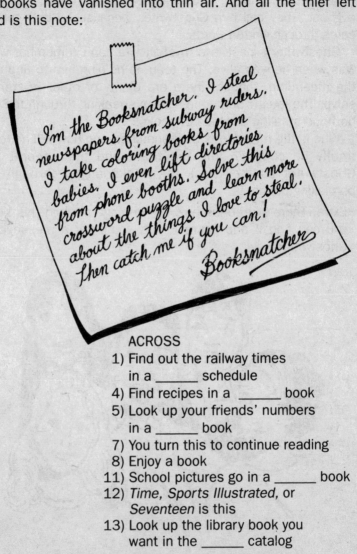

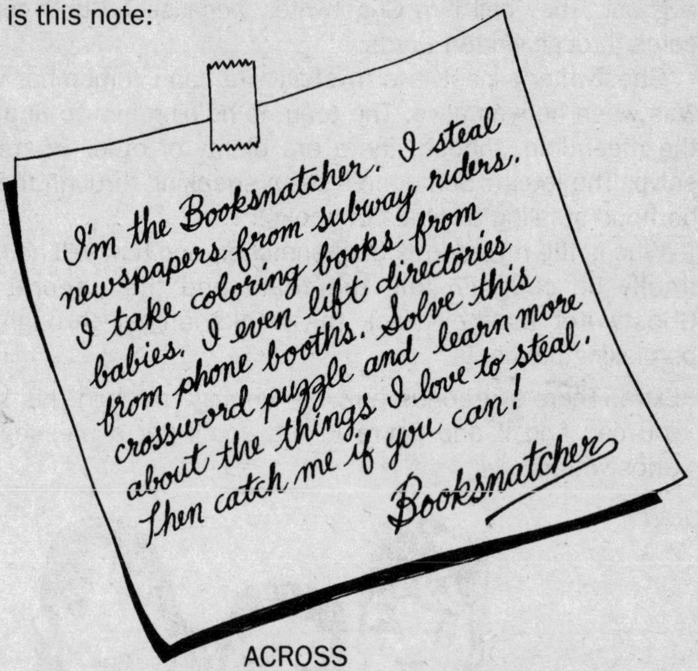
I'm the Booksnatcher. I steal newspapers from subway riders. I take coloring books from babies. I even lift directories from phone booths. Solve this crossword puzzle and learn more about the things I love to steal. Then catch me if you can!
Booksnatcher

ACROSS

1) Find out the railway times in a _____ schedule
4) Find recipes in a _____ book
5) Look up your friends' numbers in a _____ book
7) You turn this to continue reading
8) Enjoy a book
11) School pictures go in a _____ book
12) *Time, Sports Illustrated,* or *Seventeen* is this
13) Look up the library book you want in the _____ catalog

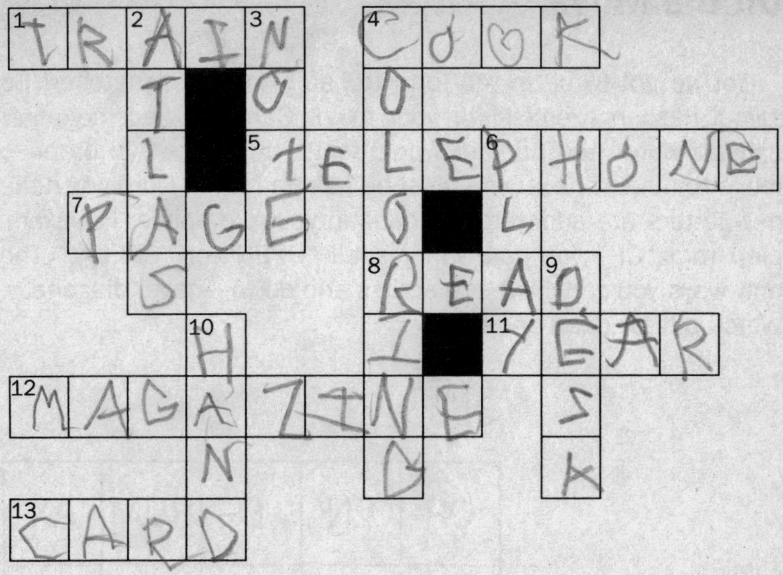

DOWN

2) A book full of maps
3) Write down clues in a ______ book
4) Use crayons to fill in a ______ book
6) Football coaches consult their ______ books
9) Sit here when you do your homework
10) You could look up ways to build a fire in a scout ______book

On the Move

You've got to be in top form to catch the Booksnatcher! So Jamal has an exercise for your mind. Can you piece together enough words to find your way through this maze? In order to move to a new space, you must be able to form a word when the new letters are added to the ones in your old space. For example, from "OP" you can either spell "OPEN" or "OPERA." The only ways you can move are across and down—never diagonally. Watch out for dead ends!

START

OP	EN	D	RUM	AX
ERA	RO	IG	BLE	ND
SE	T	LOO	SEN	DEN
VEN	OUT	P	AN	Y
T	RO	IE	GER	ES
APE	WA	STE	BIL	CAPE

FINISH

Out There, Somewhere...

Gaby has an important message for her friends. But she's written it in a secret code. Can you help decipher the message? Every letter in the code has been replaced with a different letter of the alphabet. Gaby has identified nine letters to get you started, but you'll have to use your noodle to figure out the rest.

Helpful hints:

- If you see a letter by itself, it's probably A or I, because they're the only one-letter words.
- If you have a three-letter word that begins with T H, you can be pretty sure the third letter is E!

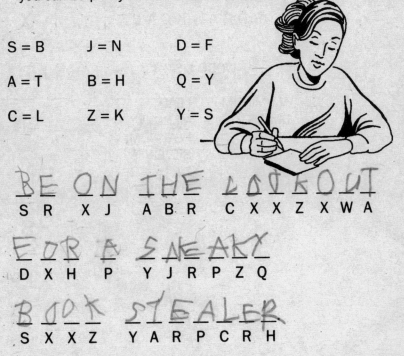

S = B	J = N	D = F
A = T	B = H	Q = Y
C = L	Z = K	Y = S

S R   X J   A B R   C X X Z X W A

D X H   P   Y J R P Z Q

S X X Z   Y A R P C R H

Digging for Clues

Ghostwriter and the team know the Booksnatcher is a thief who loves puzzles. So they hid the names of 12 precious and not-so-precious metals in this word search, hoping to trap their thief. The Booksnatcher didn't take the bait. But if you find all the words, the uncircled letters will spell the answer to a riddle.

- Look for the words in the list.
- Circle them when you find them in the puzzle.
- Words may go up, down, across, and backwards, like this:

```
P D   A C R O S S
U O
  W   S D R A W K C A B
  N
```

WORD LIST

ALUMINUM	LEAD
BRASS	MERCURY
BRONZE	PLATINUM
COPPER	SILVER
GOLD	TIN
IRON	TITANIUM

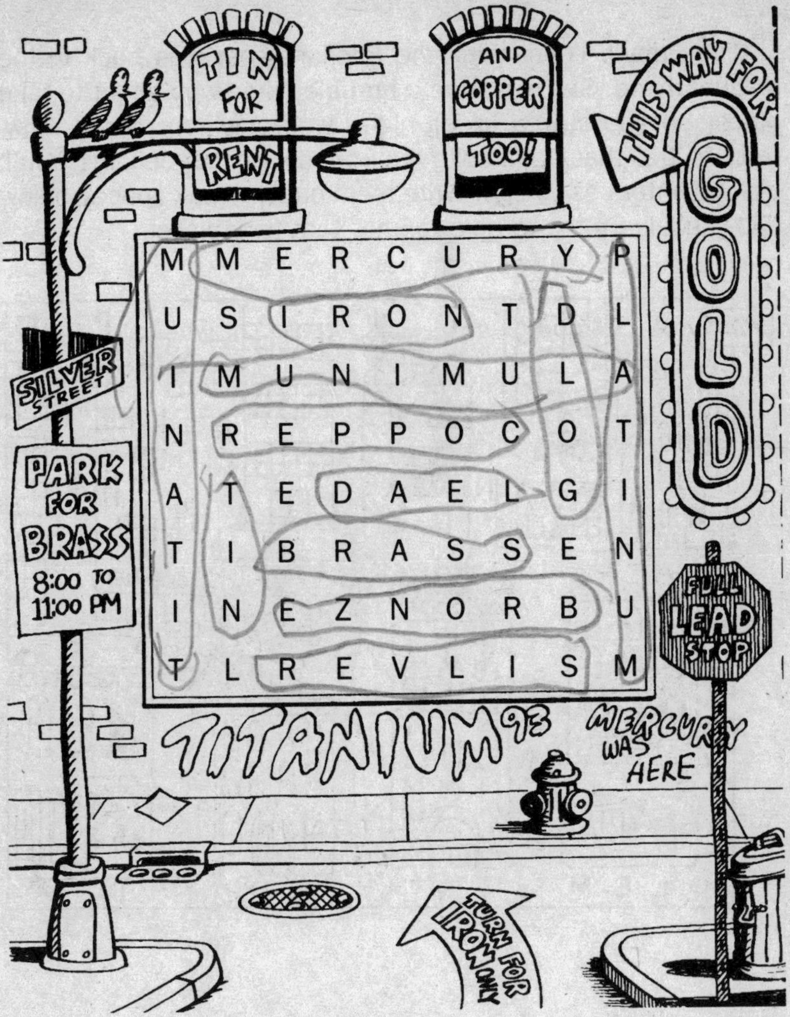

M	M	E	R	C	U	R	Y	P
U	S	I	R	O	N	T	D	L
I	M	U	N	I	M	U	L	A
N	R	E	P	P	O	C	O	T
A	T	E	D	A	E	L	G	I
T	I	B	R	A	S	S	E	N
I	N	E	Z	N	O	R	B	U
T	L	R	E	V	L	I	S	M

Now find the uncircled letters. (Look in each line from left to right and from top to bottom.) Write them on the blank spaces below to find the answer to this riddle:

WHAT'S A THIEF'S FAVORITE METAL?

STEEL

Be on the Lookout

Clues made Lenni think the Booksnatcher was back in the neighborhood. She was sure a horrible crime was about to take place. So she stayed up all night, watching from her window. Find the trail that leads up to the front door of her building. You'll pick up letters as you go. Write them on the blank spaces below and you'll learn the terrible "crime" that took place.

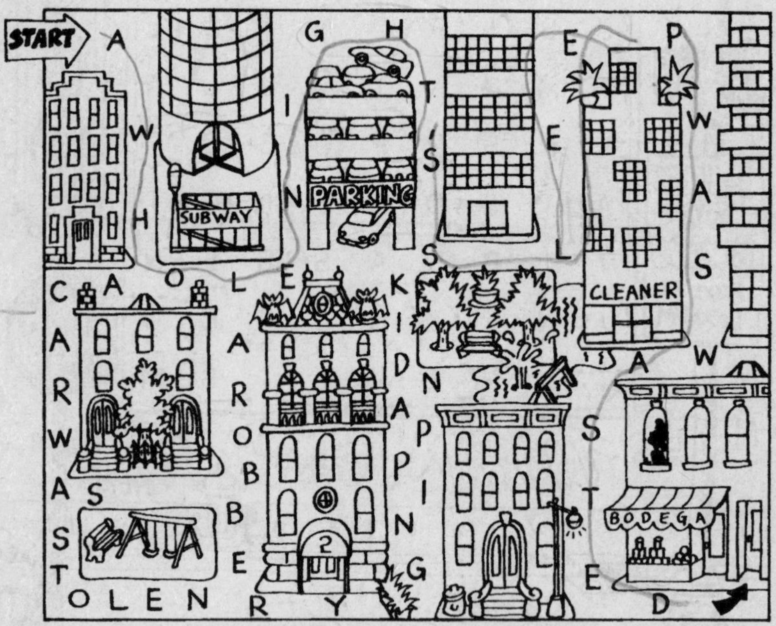

A whole night's

sleep was wasted!

You Drive Me Crazy

Jamal and Alex tracked the Booksnatcher to a parking lot, but then they lost the trail. They asked Ghostwriter if he could find any sign of the book thief. Now he's using the license plates on the back of these cars to send his friends a message. Follow the steps at the bottom of the page to find out what he is saying.

1) Use the first number on each plate to arrange them all from smallest to biggest.
2) Cross out all the X's and P's.
3) Cross out all the numbers. (Leave the O's! They're letters.)
4) Write the remaining letters on the blank spaces at the bottom of the page. Remember to start with the "smallest" license plate!
5) Read the important message from Ghostwriter.

__ __   __ __ __ __ __   __ __ __ __ __ __   __ __ __ __

Easy Riders

The Booksnatcher just hit New York's biggest bookstore—and now the Ghostwriter team has to get to the scene of the crime. Should they take the subway? The bus? A helicopter? There are so many ways to get around. How many can you find in this word search? When you're done, the leftover letters will answer a riddle.

- Look for the words in the list.
- Circle them when you find them in the puzzle.
- Words may go up, down, across, backwards, and diagonally, like this:

```
                                                   Y
                                                 L
                                               L
                                             A
P D    A C R O S S                         N
U O                                      O
  W    S D R A W K C A B               G
  N                                  A
                                   I
                                 D
```

WORD LIST

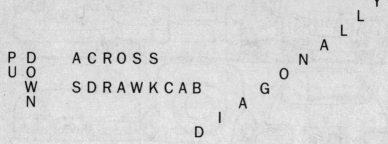

AIRPLANE	MONORAIL
BICYCLE	MOTORCYCLE
BLIMP	POGO STICK
BOAT	SLED
BUS	SUBWAY
CAMEL	TRAIN
CANOE	TRUCK
CAR	WAGON
HELICOPTER	

R	E	T	P	O	C	I	L	E	H
A	T	E	O	W	A	R	S	L	S
C	A	N	G	A	M	T	L	C	U
F	P	A	O	G	E	A	E	Y	B
N	M	L	S	O	L	O	D	C	W
I	I	P	T	N	N	B	F	R	A
A	L	R	I	A	I	C	J	O	Y
R	B	I	C	Y	C	L	E	T	B
T	A	A	K	C	U	R	T	O	U
M	L	I	A	R	O	N	O	M	S

Now find the uncircled letters. (Look in each line from left to right and from top to bottom.) Write them on the blank spaces below to find the answer to this riddle:

WHY WAS THE ROAD STICKY?

_ _ _ _ _ _ _   _ _ _

Decode These Notes

To keep their information from falling into the wrong hands, detectives often write their notes in codes. But Lenni writes her codes in notes! The Booksnatcher stole Lenni's code book—and left her a coded clue. It's on the next page.

Use the chart below to find out what letter each musical symbol stands for. Write them on the blanks on the next page and you'll learn something important about the Booksnatcher.

♩ = A	𝄢 = B	⊕ = C	ɤ = D
♪ = E	▬ = F	♭ = G	𝄞 = H
♭ = I	¢ = J	𝄪 = K	⁊ = L
♭♭ = M	⌢ = N	♮ = O	○ = P
♩ = Q	♫ = R	:‖ = S	♫ = T
↑ = U	♫♫ = V	▬ = W	♯ = X
♪. = Y	¾ = Z		

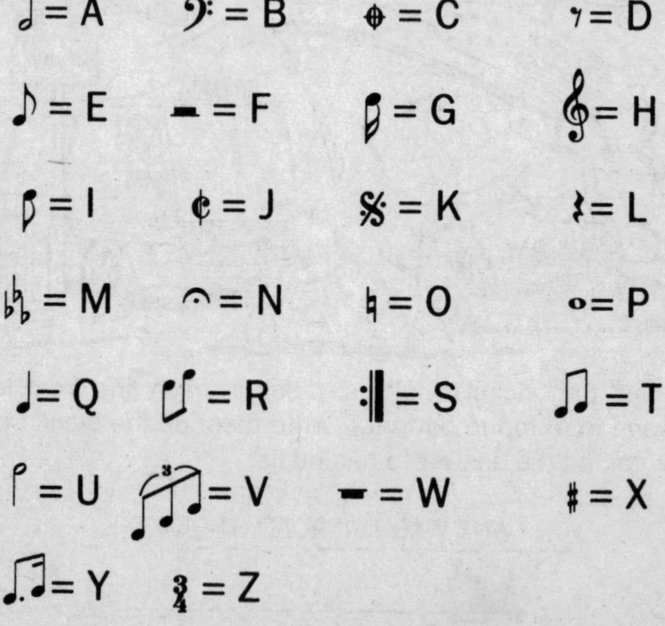

The Booksnatcher's Message

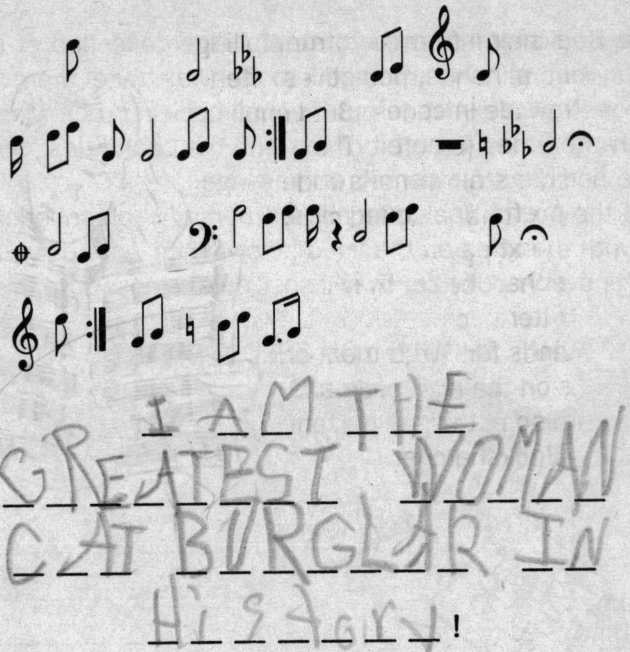

Bonus:
Now decode these notes to read the answer to Lenni's riddle:

HOW DID THE CONDUCTOR GET TO BE
IN CHARGE OF THE ORCHESTRA?

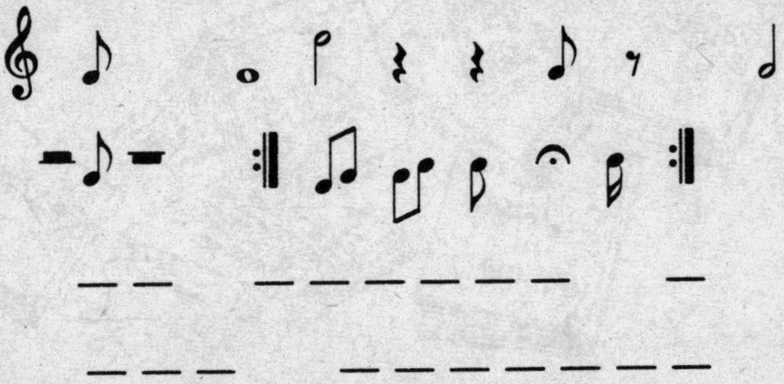

Empty Shelves

The Booksnatcher tried to steal Alex's collection of mystery novels, but all she managed to do was take them off the shelves. Now Alex has to put them all back in order. Meanwhile, Ghostwriter is having a bit of fun with the book titles. Solve this puzzle and discover his secret message.

Put the books Booksnatcher *left behind* in alphabetical order and write the titles on the lines below. Then write down the last letter of every book title. They'll spell out the answer to this riddle:

WHAT SHOULD YOU FEED A SMART BIRD?

Turn and Turn Again

Ghostwriter and Lenni made this puzzle and left it in the library. They hoped to lure the Booksnatcher to it. She never showed up, so now it's up to you to keep this great puzzle from going to waste!

Changing one letter at a time, turn the top word in each puzzle into the word at the bottom. The pictures to the right of each ladder are clues to help you fill in the missing words. To get you started, Lenni circled the letters you should change.

❶ C A L L

_ _ _ _

T A L K

❷ W O R K

_ _ _ _

_ _ _ _

F A R M

❸ B O O K

_ _ _ _

_ _ _ _

_ _ _ _

W O R D

Eat This!

Burned again! The Booksnatcher stole Lenni's father's cookbook. Max was making a very special meal, and it got ruined. Boy, was he steamed! While he stewed over the crime, Lenni cooked up this puzzle to sweeten his temper. Find the 17 kitchen items hidden in this word search.

- Look for the words in the list.
- Circle them when you find them in the puzzle.
- Words may go up, down, across, backwards, and diagonally, like this:

```
                                                      Y
                              D                     L
                                I                 L
                                  A             A
P D     A C R O S S                 G         N
U O                                     O
  W     S D R A W K C A B           G         N
  N                               A             A
                                I                 L
                              D                     L
                                                      Y
```

WORD LIST

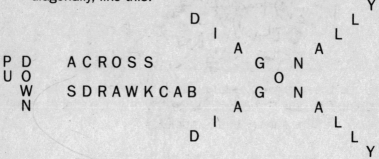

BLENDER	POT
BOWL	ROLLING PIN
COOKBOOK	SINK
CUP	SKILLET
FORK	SPOON
KNIFE	STRAINER
MIXER	TRAY
OVEN	WHISK
PAN	

N	I	P	G	N	I	L	L	O	R
M	T	O	P	T	K	P	K	R	S
I	B	O	W	L	R	O	A	E	K
X	A	L	K	L	O	A	K	N	I
E	W	N	E	B	F	S	Y	I	L
R	I	O	K	N	I	F	E	A	L
S	A	O	V	H	D	P	Y	R	E
S	O	P	W	E	U	E	B	T	T
C	A	S	C	C	N	O	R	S	N

Now find the uncircled letters. (Look in each line from left to right and from top to bottom.) Write them on the blank spaces below to find the answer to this riddle:

WHY DO PIGS MAKE GREAT CHEFS?

They're _ _ _ _ _ _ _   _ _ _ _ _ _

Casing the Joint

Jamal and Alex got a hot tip: The Booksnatcher is hiding out among the dummies in the wax museum! The problem is she's in disguise. Unscramble the names of the characters below and write them on the blank spaces. If you do it correctly, the letters in the circles, reading down, will tell which one is the Booksnatcher.

MARFRE   FAR(M)ER

RUNSE   N(U)RSE

STAROUTAN   A(S)TR(O)NAUT

APINERT   PA(I)NTER

HECF   C(H)EF

VEECTTIDE   DETEC(T)IVE

ARGOLIL   GORILL(A)

RALELABIN   BALE(R)INA

Tina Translates

The Ghostwriter team has just discovered a collection of mysterious messages. Tina thinks the Booksnatcher may have left them. They're all words or sayings that you've heard before, but they've been written out in a mixed-up manner.

Tina's figured out the first message. It says "You are under arrest." Get it?

Now see if you can decipher the other mixed-up messages.

❶ ARREST / U R (ARREST printed above a line, U R below it)

❷ CRI PARTNERS ME

❸ The WAKE UP Night (WAKE printed above UP)

❹
CLUE
DIG CLUE
CLUE
CLUE

❺
T
H
E
CROOK

❻ FOR MISSING MATION

In the Bag

The team is heading out into the field to track down clues about the Booksnatcher. Nobody knows how iong this is going to take, so they're bringing bag lunches along. Solve this puzzle to help them pack. Fit the foods from the word list into the diagram. Ghostwriter has put some letters in place to get you started.

WORD LIST

APPLE
BEEF
CARROT
CHEESE
COOKIES
FLOUR
HOT DOGS
LEMONS
PEAR
PIE
RICE
SUGAR
SYRUP

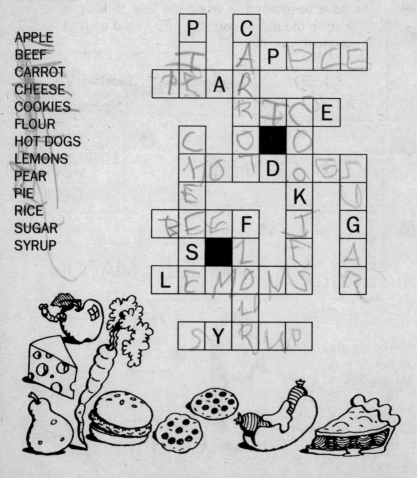

Very Vexing

The Booksnatcher has dodged the team! Gaby is frustrated, but Ghostwriter has this tip for her: When solving mysteries it may often seem as if you are going around in circles. But remember, everything is connected.

With Ghostwriter's advice in mind, solve this circular puzzle. Write one word in every space of this circle. Each word can only have one letter different from either of the words next to it. A few words have been filled in along the way to keep you on track. If you solve the puzzle correctly, you'll wind up right back where you started!

Eye Spy

Gaby and Lenni need a break from trying to catch the Booksnatcher. So, with some help from Ghostwriter, they made up this crossword. Solve it and see how good a detective you are.

ACROSS

1. Secret agent
4. Private _____
6. Search _____ clues
9. Gets better
10. New England state famous for lobsters
11. Hearing organ
12. Police officer
13. Allow
14. Initials for Drug Enforcement Agency
16. Make a knot
18. Banana _____
19. Had dinner
20. Extrasensory perception, for short
22. Automobile
24. These letters are a call for help
26. Adam and _____
28. Model airplane sets
30. Words from some ghosts
31. _____ and tell
33. Cried
34. The Spanish word for "moon"
35. Not doing anything
36. Not him
37. It shines during the day
38. Short for earned run average

DOWN

1. Master detective Holmes
2. Tiny green vegetable
3. Scotland _____
4. Gets away
5. Takes everything out of
6. A dossier is a secret _____
7. Three minus two
8. Goes back over a trail
15. Abbreviation for Eastern Standard Time
17. Contraction of "it is"
19. King _____ and his knights of the Round Table
21. There are more than 5 billion of these in the world
23. Pathway in a supermarket
25. Opposite of "off"
27. Person who chooses a candidate in an election
29. Male child
30. Place to sleep
32. Past tense of "is"
33. Be victorious

Stealing Time

When the Booksnatcher broke into Mr. and Mrs. Ferguson's party store and stole all the birthday cards, she forgot to use an important object. Now the Ghostwriter team has some valuable knowledge about her. Use the word list below to find all the tools that the thief used. The one item *not* in the word search is the one that she forgot.

- Look for the words in the list.
- Circle them when you find them in the puzzle.
- Words may go up, down, across, and backwards, like this:

```
P D   A C R O S S
U O
  W   S D R A W K C A B
  N
```

WORD LIST

AXE	PICK
CHISEL	PLIERS
CLAMP	PUTTY
FILE	SAW
GLOVES	STRING
HAMMER	TAPE
KNIFE	WIRE
NEEDLE	WRENCH

E	P	A	T	F	I	N	C	P	S
L	W	R	E	N	C	H	H	U	R
D	G	E	R	P	L	A	I	T	E
E	E	R	I	I	A	M	S	T	I
E	L	P	W	C	M	M	E	Y	L
N	I	R	I	K	P	E	L	N	P
E	F	I	N	K	T	R	A	X	E
S	T	R	I	N	G	S	W	A	S

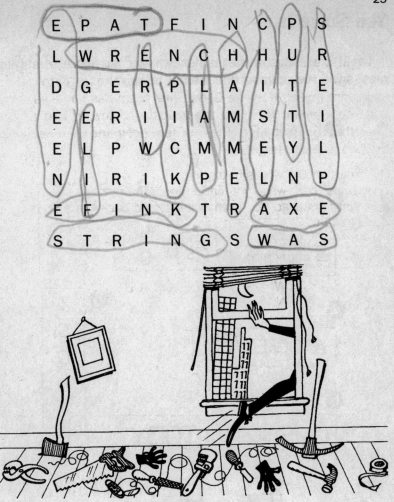

Find the one item in the word list that isn't in the puzzle. Got it? That's the item the thief forgot to use. Now find the uncircled letters. (Look in each line from left to right and from top to bottom.) They'll tell you what new info the team got about the master thief.

FINGERPRINTS

You Solve It

Look! The Ghostwriter team has found six more mystifying messages. Alex can decode them. Can you?

1

Mr. E

2

L
C E
U C U
L S
E S
C
L
E U
S

3

U R
———
SUSPICION

4

AAGGEENNTT

5

!
S
D
N
A
H

6

CUS SUSPECT TODY

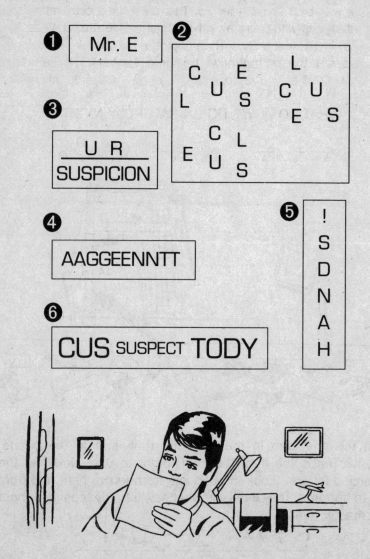

On Ice

The Ghostwriter Team has trapped the Booksnatcher! They've got her locked in the storeroom at the bodega, and the police are on their way over to pick her up. This calls for a celebration! So celebrate along with them by solving this festive puzzle. Write the answers next to each clue. Then copy the numbered letters onto the spaces at the top that have the same numbers. (The team did one for you.) When you're done, you'll get the answer to this riddle:

WHAT DO COWS DO ON SATURDAY NIGHT?

$\underline{T}_1 \underline{H}_2 \underline{E}_3 \underline{Y}_4 \quad \underline{G}_5 \underline{O}_6 \quad \underline{T}_7 \underline{O}_8$

$\underline{T}_9 \underline{H}_{10} \underline{E}_{11} \quad \underline{M}_{12} \underline{O}_{13} \underline{O}_{14} - \underline{V}_{15} \underline{I}_{16} \underline{E}_{17} \underline{S}_{18}$

1) Toy on a string.............................. $\underline{Y}_4 \underline{O}_{13} - \underline{Y}_{?} \underline{O}_8$

2) _____ or later.............................. $\underline{S} \underline{O}_{14} \underline{O}_6 \underline{N} \underline{E}_3 \underline{R}$

3) Always brush these after eating.... $\underline{\ }_9 - \underline{\ }_{17} \underline{\ }_7 \underline{\ }_2$

4) Scrabble or checkers .... $\underline{\ }_5 - \underline{\ }_{12} -$

5) Popular song or movie.................. $\underline{\ }_{10} \underline{\ }_{16} \underline{\ }_1$

6) Grapes grow on these .... $\underline{\ }_{15} - - \underline{\ }_{11} \underline{\ }_{18}$

Unlocked Door

Oh, no! While the team was celebrating, the Booksnatcher picked the lock and escaped! To make matters worse, Alex's atlas is missing. Is the Booksnatcher using it to plan an escape route? Has she left the country? She could be anywhere!

There are 15 places hidden below. (Let's hope that the Booksnatcher hasn't fled to any of them.) Find them and then find the answer to Alex's riddle.

- Look for the words in the list.
- Circle them when you find them in the puzzle.
- Words may go up, down, across, backwards, and diagonally, like this:

```
                                                  Y
                           D                    L
                             I                L
                               A            A
P D    A C R O S S               G        N
U O                                 O
  W    S D R A W K C A B         G        N
  N                            A            A
                             I                L
                           D                    L
                                                  Y
```

WORD LIST

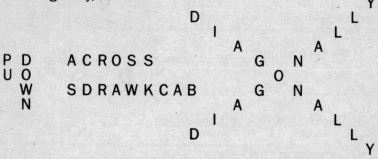

BRAZIL	ISRAEL
CANADA	JAPAN
CHINA	MADAGASCAR
CUBA	MEXICO
FRANCE	PERU
GREECE	TOGO
INDIA	ZAIRE
IRAQ	

L	F	T	O	G	O	U	B	E	C
I	R	A	U	S	R	A	C	E	I
Z	A	I	R	E	O	I	H	C	S
A	N	T	P	C	U	D	I	A	R
R	C	R	I	E	K	N	N	N	A
B	E	X	E	E	Y	I	A	A	E
W	E	A	S	R	C	P	R	D	L
M	A	D	A	G	A	S	C	A	R
C	U	B	A	J	H	I	L	E	Q

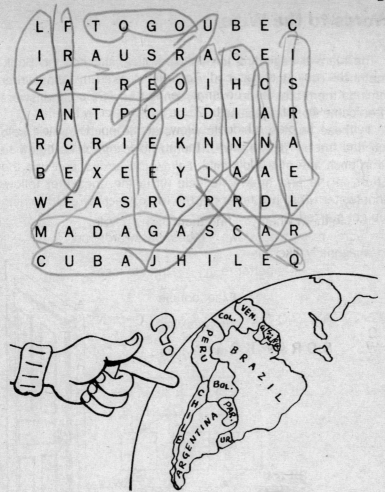

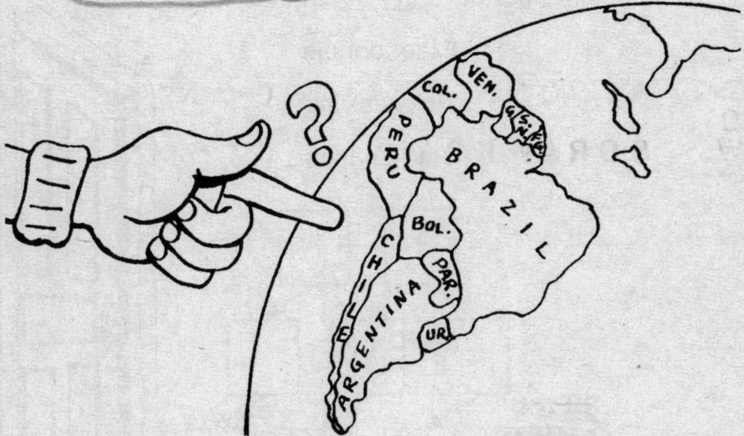

Now find the uncircled letters. (Look in each line from left to right and from top to bottom.) Write them on the blank spaces below to find the answer to this riddle:

WHY WAS THE COLD THANKSGIVING
DINNER LIKE A MESSED-UP MAP?

_ _ _ _ _ _ _   _ _ _ _ _ _

_ _ _   _ _ _ _ _

Words to the Wise

The team is beginning to think they'll never catch the Booksnatcher. They only have a few little clues! But Ghostwriter reminds them that when you're solving a mystery, big answers often come from little clues.

In these puzzles, the little words at the beginning will help you find the big answers at the end. Solve the clues below to fill in each line of the pyramid. Follow the arrows and use the letters in the first answer to help fill in the ones that follow. Ghostwriter wrote two letters at the top of each pyramid to help you get started.

1

It's better to ______ than to lose

Exact double

Heavy string

Cold season

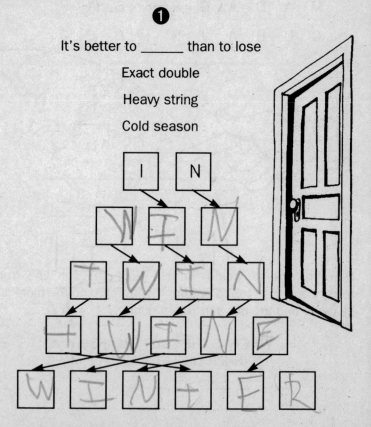

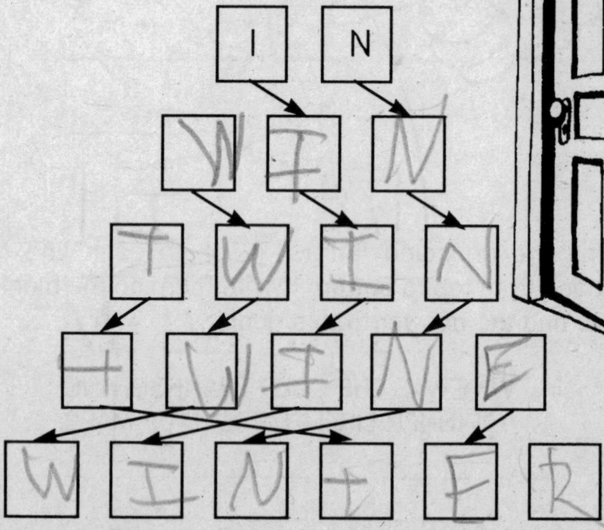

❷

2,000 pounds

Short letter

Rock

What a robber's stuff is

Idaho to Iowa

Lieutenant McQuade just called with some important information: The Booksnatcher has definitely not left the country. Of course, that still leaves a wide area to cover. Fortunately, Ghostwriter has found some extra information in the jumbled letters on the next page. Unscramble the names of the 13 states and write them on the blank spaces. If you do it correctly, the letters in the circles, reading down, will spell out Ghostwriter's news. (He's filled in the first letter of each state's name for you.)

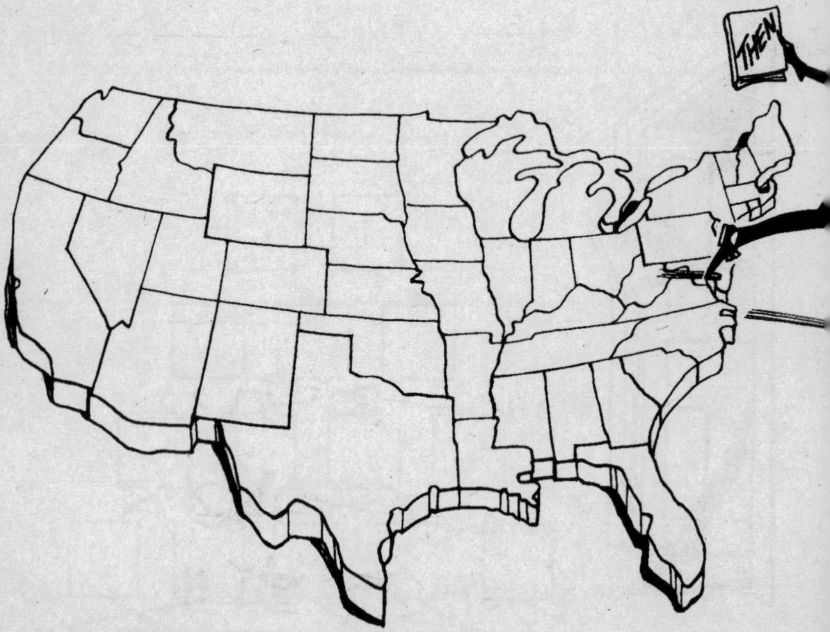

SNASAK	K _ _ _ _ _
HAUT	U _ _ _
GROGAEI	G _ _ _ _ _ _
ALAINSIOU	L _ _ _ _ _ _ _ _
DROFILA	F _ _ _ _ _ _
REWADALE	D _ _ _ _ _ _ _
MABALAA	A _ _ _ _ _ _
FLIROAINAC	C _ _ _ _ _ _ _ _ _
DROALOOC	C _ _ _ _ _ _ _
BASKENAR	N _ _ _ _ _ _ _
KASALA	A _ _ _ _ _
HAGNOTWISN	W _ _ _ _ _ _ _ _ _
CUTENKYK	K _ _ _ _ _ _ _

New Look

Alex found out that the Booksnatcher is casing the book stalls on Fifth Avenue, by Central Park. This time the Ghostwriter team is not going to let her get away! However, the crook is wearing yet another disguise. So roll up your sleeves and solve another mysterious word search. Hats off to you if you can find 14 things you might wear as part of a disguise.

- Look for the words in the list.
- Circle them when you find them in the puzzle.
- Words may go up, down, across, backwards, and diagonally, like this:

```
                                                        Y
                              D                       L
                                I                   L
                                  A               A
P D      A C R O S S                G           N
U O                                       O
  W      S D R A W K C A B          G           N
  N                               A               A
                                I                   L
                              D                       L
                                                        Y
```

WORD LIST

DRESS	SHIRT
GLOVES	SHOES
HAT	SKIRT
MAKEUP	SWEATER
MASK	TROUSERS
OVERCOAT	VEST
SCARF	WIG

G	L	O	V	E	S	S	S	S	T
S	M	W	O	C	S	H	K	C	S
W	A	K	I	E	E	S	I	A	E
E	S	A	O	G	R	N	R	R	V
A	K	H	D	B	D	E	T	F	T
T	S	R	E	S	U	O	R	T	A
E	L	M	A	K	E	U	P	T	H
R	S	O	V	E	R	C	O	A	T

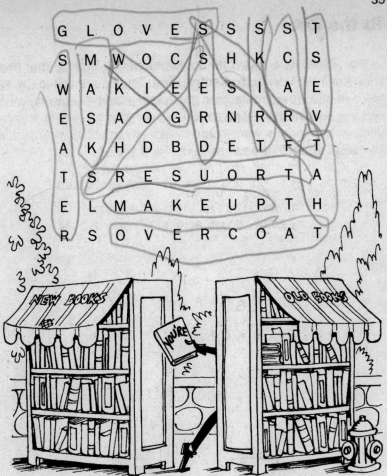

Now find the uncircled letters. (Look in each line from left to right and from top to bottom.) Write them on the blank spaces below to find the answer to this riddle:

WHAT KIND OF CLOTHES HURT THE MOST?

______ ___ ______

To the Zoo!

The team has tracked the Booksnatcher to the Central Park Zoo. But now they have to figure out where she's hiding! So enjoy this word search safari. If you circle all 18 animals, you'll find the answer to a riddle, too!

- Look for the words in the list.
- Circle them when you find them in the puzzle.
- Words may go up, down, across, backwards, and diagonally, like this:

Y
D L
I L
A A
P D ACROSS G N
U O O
W SDRAWKCAB G N
N A A
I L
D L
Y

WORD LIST

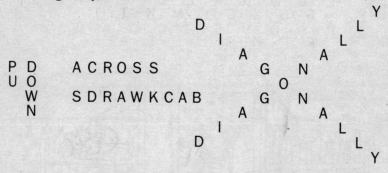

BEAR	GOPHER
CAMEL	HARE
CHIPMUNK	LIZARD
COBRA	OWL
EAGLE	PIG
ELEPHANT	PORCUPINE
FOX	TURTLE
FROG	WALRUS
GNU	WHALE

E	L	A	H	W	H	C	E	E
A	I	W	A	A	G	H	N	L
G	Z	P	R	L	O	I	E	E
L	A	I	E	R	P	P	L	P
E	R	G	N	U	H	M	T	H
A	D	S	C	S	E	U	R	A
A	G	R	O	A	R	N	U	N
F	O	X	B	C	M	K	T	T
P	R	H	R	E	B	E	A	R
E	F	T	A	A	O	W	L	H

Now find the uncircled letters. (Look in each line from left to right and from top to bottom.) Write them on the blank spaces below to find the answer to this riddle:

WHY WAS THE CAT KICKED OUT OF THE GAME?

__ __   __ __ __   __   __ __ __ __ __ __ __ __

Heaps of Hints

It's time for the Ghostwriter team to spread out in hopes of netting the notorious Booksnatcher. And it's time for you to solve another pair of puzzles that start small and spread out across the page. Solve the clues below to fill in each line of the pyramid. Follow the arrows and use the letters in the first answer to help fill in the answers that follow.

1

Use a chair

Mix with a spoon

Cars need four of these

Feature on a zebra

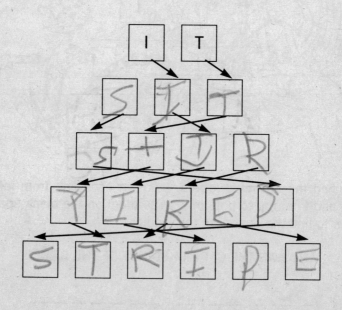

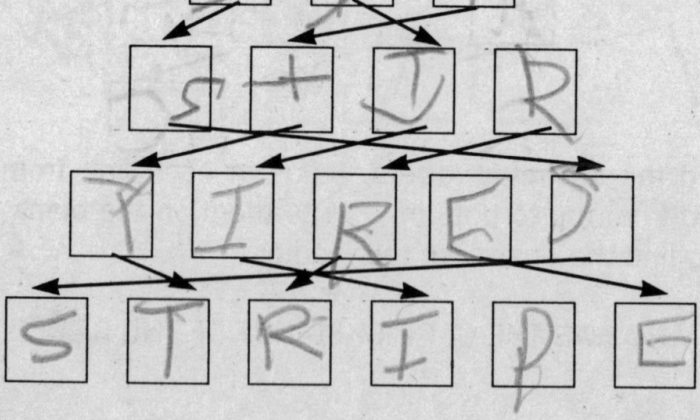

❷

Head covering

Small talk

Get the ball

Take care of an itch

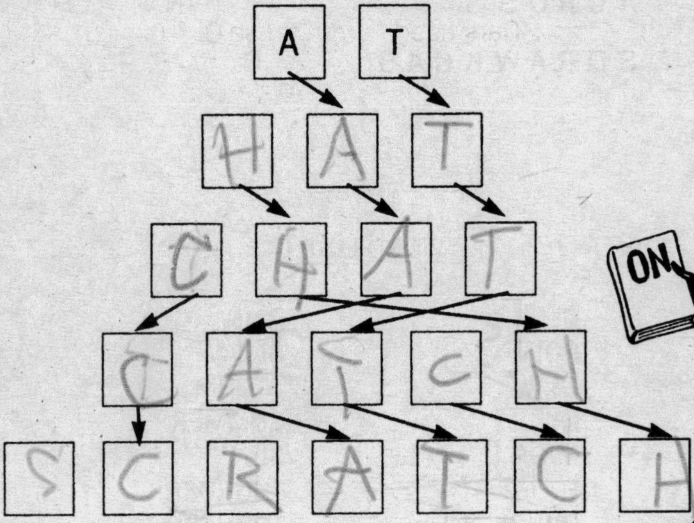

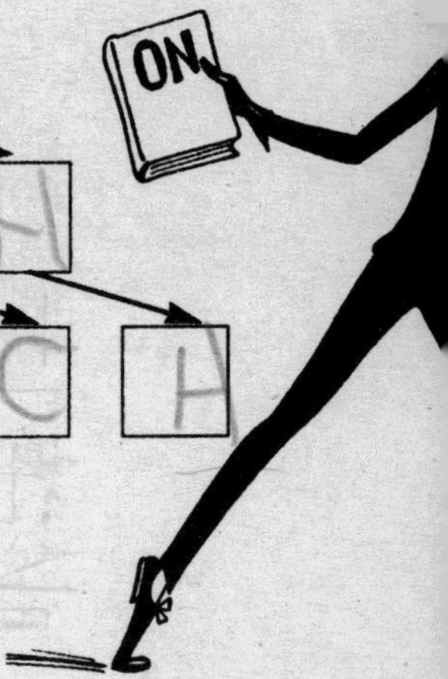

Inside Track

Jamal was stuck inside during a rainstorm while the Booksnatcher was getting away. But when the rain let up, Jamal found a new clue to track down that sneaky thief. Solve this puzzle and find out what it is.

- Look for the words in the list.
- Circle them when you find them in the puzzle.
- Words may go up, down, across, backwards, and diagonally, like this:

```
                                                  Y
                                                L
                                              L
                                            A
P D    A C R O S S                        N
U O                                     O
  W    S D R A W K C A B              G
  N                                 A
                                  I
                                D
```

WORD LIST

CLOUD	RAIN
COLD	SNOW
DEW	STORM
FALL	SUMMER
FOG	SUN
FROST	THUNDER
HURRICANE	TORNADO
ICE	WARM
LIGHTNING	WIND
MOON	WINTER

T	M	S	T	O	R	M	U	D	R	R	D
O	D	L	O	C	D	Y	N	E	F	A	S
R	E	M	M	U	S	I	T	D	R	I	U
N	W	O	N	S	W	N	U	F	O	N	N
A	M	O	O	N	I	O	O	O	S	T	W
D	P	R	I	W	L	L	A	F	T	F	A
O	E	N	A	C	I	R	R	U	H	O	R
L	I	G	H	T	N	I	N	G	N	G	M
R	E	D	N	U	H	T	E	C	I	T	S

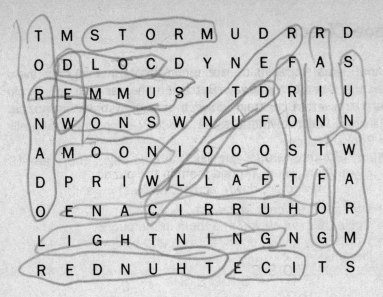

Now find the uncircled letters. (Look in each line from left to right and from top to bottom.) Write them on the blank spaces below to find the clue the Booksnatcher left behind.

_ _ _ _ _   _ _ _ _ _ _ _ _ _ _

Shoe Clue

Aha! Jamal found a trail of muddy footprints leading away from the DeKalb Avenue newsstand, the scene of the Booksnatcher's latest crime. If you can help him solve this puzzle, he'll know which of these three shadowy suspects is actually the Booksnatcher.

First, solve the word search on the next page. There are 10 kinds of footwear hidden there.

- Look for the words in the list.
- Circle them when you find them in the puzzle.
- Words may go up, down, across, and backwards, like this:

```
P D   A C R O S S
U O
  W   S D R A W K C A B
  N
```

WORD LIST

BOOTS	SANDALS
CLEATS	SKATES
CLOGS	SKIS
HIGH HEELS	SLIPPERS
PUMPS	SNEAKERS

H	S	L	A	D	N	A	S	C
S	S	U	M	O	S	U	L	S
R	L	S	G	O	L	C	E	K
E	I	O	C	Y	S	E	E	I
K	P	V	L	S	K	O	H	S
A	P	L	E	P	A	I	H	T
E	E	A	A	M	T	S	G	O
N	R	I	T	U	E	L	I	O
S	S	I	S	P	S	H	H	B

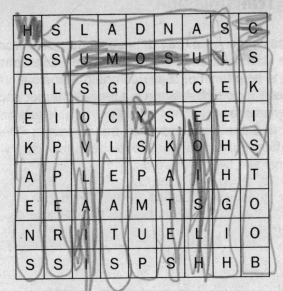

Now shade in all of the boxes that contain uncircled letters. Compare the pattern to the shoeprints above, and you'll be able to see who left the telltale trail.

Tricky Transmission

The Ghostwriter team found this coded message on Jamal's computer screen. It may be a clue from the Booksnatcher, but you need to help them decode it in order to find out!

To decode it, you must figure out a new letter for each one on the screen. Ghostwriter has identified nine letters to get you started, but the rest is up to you!

Hint: After you've filled in Ghostwriter's letters, try to figure out the one- and two-letter words.

Q = H   R = D   J = M
Z = T   C = G   D = C
X = S   G = R   A = N

WHY DID THE STINGER
BQS ROR ZQY XOACYG

CURL HIMSELF AROUND
DEGF QOJXYFK LGMEAR

A PIECE OF GUM
L NOYDY MK CEJ ?

HE WANTED TO BE
QY BLAZYR ZM TY

A RAPPER
L GLNNYG !

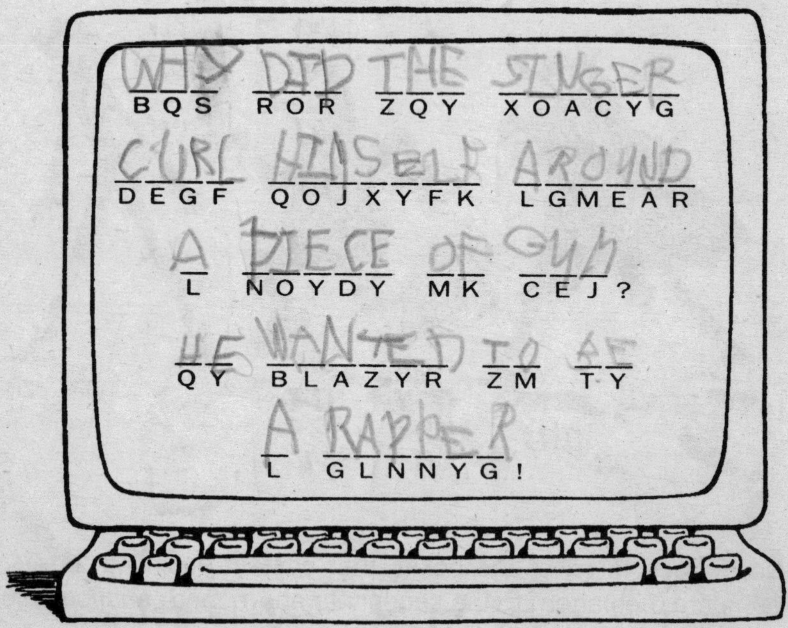

It's a Tough One

The Booksnatcher left this grid of letter blocks at the Community Center. In order to catch her, the Ghostwriter team has to make its way through the blocks. But the kids have to follow the Booksnatcher's rules! Can you help them solve this super stumper?

Find a path from start to finish. Here's the catch: You can move through as many blocks as you like, but you may only use a total of 10 different letters. You can move up, down, or across, but not diagonally.

To help you, Ghostwriter has written out the alphabet to keep track of the letters you use:

A B C D E F G H I J K L M N O P Q R S T U V W X Y Z

Made It!

Got her! The Booksnatcher thought the team would never crack her block puzzle, but she didn't count on them getting help from *you.* Now that the thief is being brought to justice, everyone's clamoring to get back their stolen property. It turns out the Booksnatcher was stealing a lot more than just books!

To solve this crossword puzzle, read each quotation and write in the person who is probably saying it.

ACROSS

1) "I want my brushes and my canvases back!"

3) "Our entire collection of mystery novels is missing —and they were never checked out!"

7) "My stethoscope! She stole my stethoscope!"

9) "I would have tracked her down by now, but it's duck season, not Booksnatcher season."

11) "I want my marionette back—no strings attached!"

12) "The voters are very upset about all the booksnatching in this district. And I'd like all my campaign posters back!"

13) "When I'm not putting out forest fires, I like to sit down with a good book. But all my books are gone—and so's my Smokey the Bear sign!"

14) "My lines! How am I supposed to learn my lines if I don't have my script?"

DOWN

1) "Hey! Who took the wings off my airplane?"

2) "I won't be able to assign any homework if I don't get my lesson books back."

4) "How can I cut hair without my scissors and comb?"

5) "It's even colder and lonelier in space without my spacesuit."

6) "I'd pin that Booksnatcher to the mat if I could get her into the ring. Grrr!"

7) "Where's the cat who stole my bongos and high hat?"

8) "I'll go down with my ship —but not without my logbooks and compass!"

10) "I'll get my tractor back, by cracky, or my name's not Old MacDonald!"

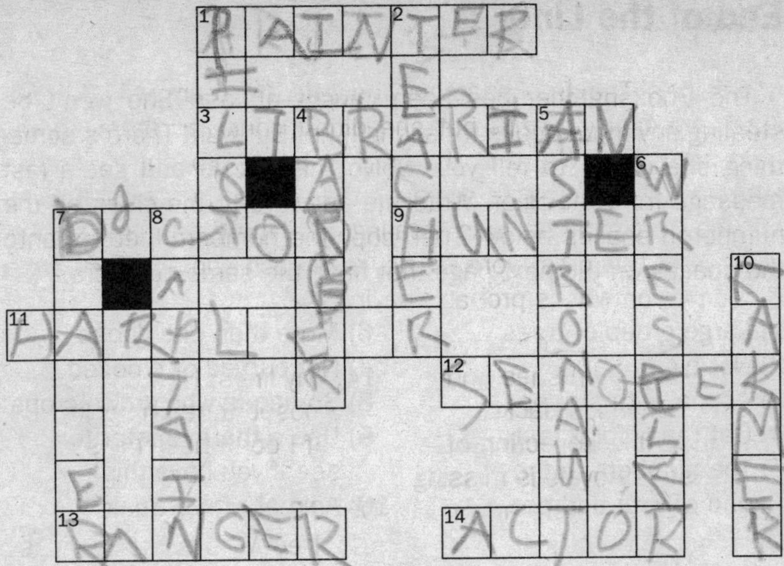

VOTE FOR
VOTE FOR ME

End of the Line

The Booksnatcher has been caught at last. She won't be stealing any more books for a long time. But wait! There's something she wants to tell you. Solve this puzzle and get a last message from the thief. Write the answers to the clues on the numbered spaces below. Then copy the numbered letters onto the spaces on the next page that have the same numbers.

1) Large group of trees
2) Not big
3) Animal with stripes
4) Get ready for a test
5) The numbers at the end of your address

6) More than one goose
7) Not curved or crooked
8) Someone who grows crops
9) Use a thermometer to see if you have this
10) Animal with a trunk

1) F O R E S T
   8 19 44 36 50 16

2) L I T T L E
   30   5 15 35 42

3) Z E B R A
   28 53   24 3

4) S T U D Y
   11 32 27   25

5) Z I P C O D E
   29 9   43 38 4 21

6) G E E S E
   52 2 17 41 31

7) S T R A I G H T
   49 12 1 40 33   6 46

8) F A R M E R
   20 51 39 47 7 18

9) L O V E R Y
   37 45 22 14 10

10) E L E P H A N T
    23 13 48 26   34

READ The First

_ _ _ _   _ _ _   _ _ _ _ _
1 2 3 4   5 6 7   8 9 10 11 12

_ _ _ _ _ _   _ _   _ _ _ _ _
13 14 15 16 17 18   19 20   21 22 23 24 25

_ _ _ _ _ _   _ _ _ _ _   _ _ _
26 27 28 29 30 31   32 33 34 35 36   37 38 39

_   _ _ _ _ _ _   _ _ _ _ _ _
40   41 42 43 44 45 46   47 48 50 51 52 53

Now follow the directions and write the correct letters onto the spaces below to read the Booksnatcher's final message.

_ _ _ _ _ _ _ _ _ _, _ _ _ _ _ _ _ _ _ _ _ _ _ _. _ _ _ _

_ _ _   _   _ _ _ _ _   _ _ _ _ _!

Answers

Greetings, Detectives!

On the Move

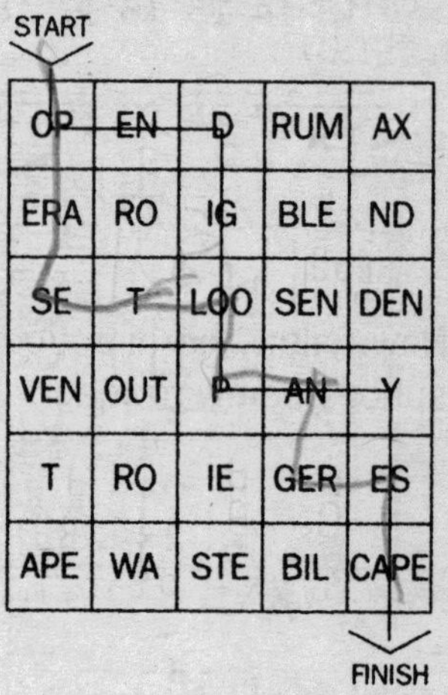

Out There, Somewhere...

Gaby's secret message says: BE ON THE LOOK-OUT FOR A SNEAKY BOOK STEALER

Digging for Clues

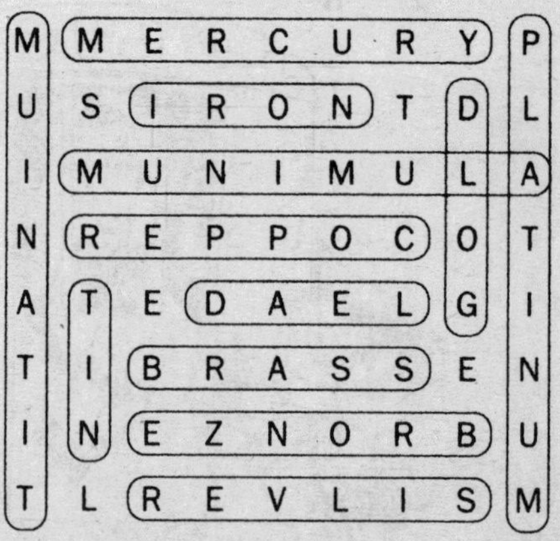

Answer to riddle: STEEL

Be on the Lookout

The correct path spells out this message: A WHOLE NIGHT'S SLEEP WAS WASTED

You Drive Me Crazy

Ghostwriter's secret message says: NO BOOKS AROUND HERE

Easy Riders

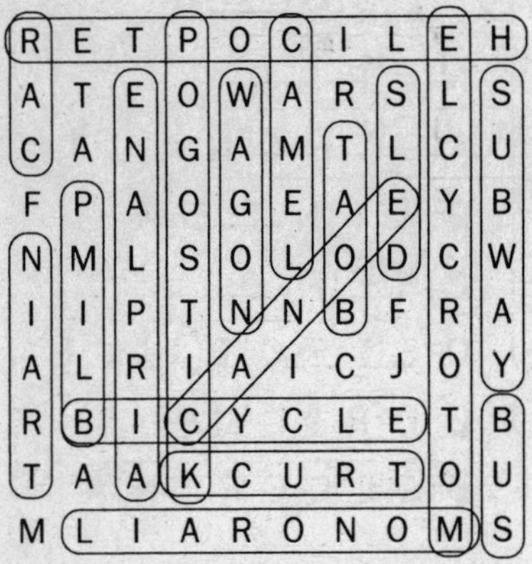

Answer to riddle: TRAFFIC JAM

Decode These Notes

The Booksnatcher's message says: I AM THE GREATEST WOMAN CAT BURGLAR IN HISTORY

The answer to Lenni's riddle is: HE PULLED A FEW STRINGS

Empty Shelves

Titles:
Amy and the Giant Rhubarb
And Then There Were Zero
Decision at Kalamazoo
Encyclopedia Black
From the Cluttered Desk of
Basil F. Marshmallow
Hardly Boys and Nancy Who
Jack the Zipper
Sherlock Foam
Walruses on the Orient Express

What should you feed a smart bird?
Answer: BOOKWORMS

Eat This!

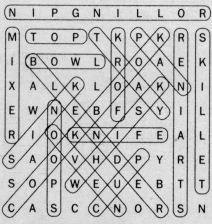

N	I	P	G	N	I	L	L	O	R
M	T	O	P	T	K	P	K	R	S
I	B	O	W	L	R	O	A	E	K
X	A	L	K	L	O	A	K	N	I
E	W	N	E	B	F	S	Y	I	L
R	I	O	K	N	I	F	E	A	L
S	A	O	V	H	D	P	Y	R	E
S	O	P	W	E	U	E	B	T	T
C	A	S	C	C	N	O	R	S	N

Answer to riddle:
They're ALWAYS BACON

Turn and Turn Again

1) C A L L
T A L L
T A L K

2) W O R K
W O R M
W A R M
F A R M

3) B O O K
C O O K
C O R K
C O R D
W O R D

Casing the Joint

F A R M E R
N U R S E
A S T R O N A U T
P A I N T E R
C H E F
D E T E C T I V E
G O R I L L A
B A L L E R I N A

The Booksnatcher is disguised as a MUSICIAN.

Tina Translates

1) You are under arrest

2) Partners in crime

3) Wake up in the middle of the night

4) Dig for clues

5) Corner the crook

6) Missing information

In the Bag

Very Vexing

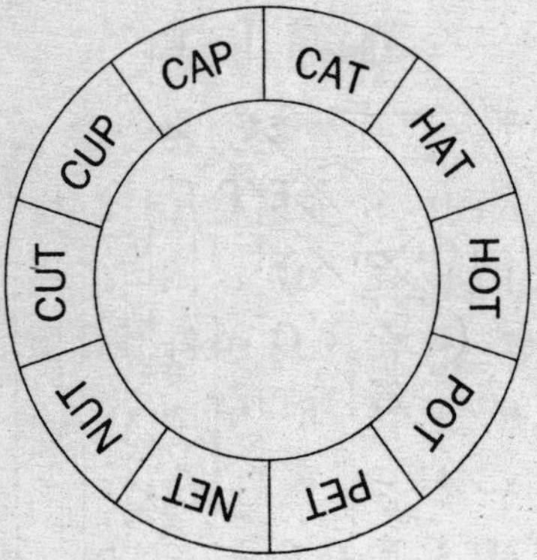

Eye Spy

S	P	Y		E	Y	E		F	O	R
H	E	A	L	S		M	A	I	N	E
E	A	R		C	O	P		L	E	T
R		D	E	A		T	I	E		R
L			S	P	L	I	T			A
O		A	T	E		E	S	P		C
C	A	R		S	O	S		E	V	E
K	I	T	S		N		B	O	O	S
	S	H	O	W		W	E	P	T	
	L	U	N	A		I	D	L	E	
H	E	R		S	U	N		E	R	A

Stealing Time

E	P	A	T	F	I	N	C	P	S
L	W	R	E	N	C	H	H	U	R
D	G	E	R	P	L	A	I	T	E
E	E	R	I	I	A	M	S	T	I
E	L	P	W	C	M	M	E	Y	L
N	I	R	I	K	P	E	L	N	P
E	F	I	N	K	T	R	A	X	E
S	T	R	I	N	G	S	W	A	S

The item not found in the word search is GLOVES. The thief left FINGERPRINTS at the scene of the crime.

You Solve It

1) Mystery

2) Scrambled clues

3) You are above suspicion

4) Double agent

5) Hands up!

6) Suspect in custody

On Ice

1) Yo-yo

2) Sooner

3) Teeth

4) Game

5) Hit

6) Vines

What do cows do on Saturday night? THEY GO TO THE MOO-VIES

Unlocked Door

L	F	T	O	G	O	U	B	E	C
I	R	A	U	S	R	A	C	E	I
Z	A	I	R	E	O	I	H	C	S
A	N	T	P	C	U	D	I	A	R
R	C	R	I	E	K	N	N	N	A
B	E	X	E	E	Y	I	A	A	E
W	E	A	S	R	C	P	R	D	L
M	A	D	A	G	A	S	C	A	R
C	U	B	A	J	H	I	L	E	Q

Answer to riddle: BECAUSE TURKEY WAS CHILE

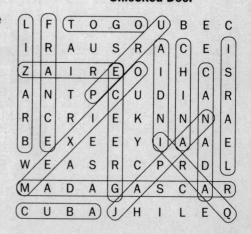

Words to the Wise

❶

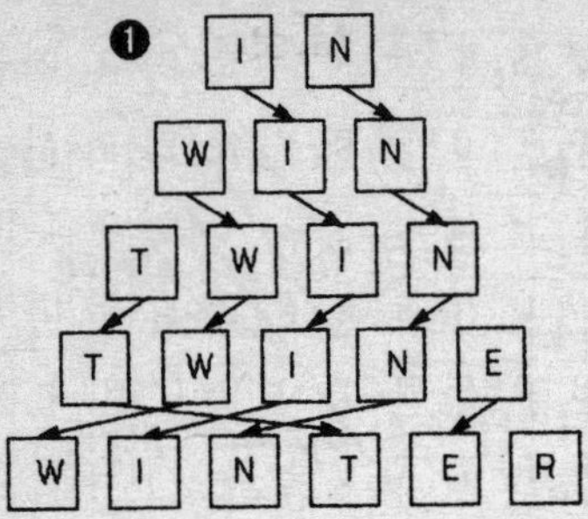

❷

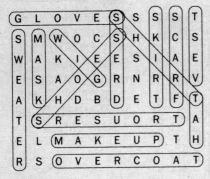

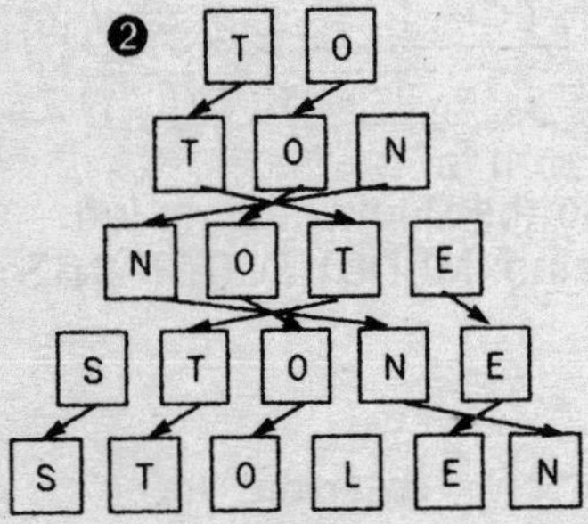

Idaho to Iowa

K A N S A S
U T A H
G E O R G I A
L O U I S I A N A
F L O R I D A
D E L A W A R E
A L A B A M A
C A L I F O R N I A
C O L O R A D O
N E B R A S K A
A L A S K A
W A S H I N G T O N
K E N T U C K Y

Ghostwriter's message says:
SHE IS A FEW MILES AWAY

New Look

G	L	O	V	E	S	S	S	S	T
S	M	W	O	C	S	H	K	C	S
W	A	K	I	E	E	S	I	A	E
E	S	A	O	G	R	N	R	R	V
A	K	H	D	B	D	E	T	F	T
T	S	R	E	S	U	O	R	T	A
E	L	M	A	K	E	U	P	T	H
R	S	O	V	E	R	C	O	A	T

Answer to riddle: SOCKS AND BELTS

To the Zoo!

E	L	A	H	W	H	C	E	E
A	I	W	A	A	G	H	N	L
G	Z	P	R	L	O	I	E	E
L	A	I	E	R	P	P	L	P
E	R	G	N	U	H	M	T	H
A	D	S	C	S	E	U	R	A
A	G	R	O	A	R	N	U	N
F	O	X	B	C	M	K	T	T
P	R	H	R	E	B	E	A	R
E	F	T	A	A	O	W	L	H

Answer to riddle: HE WAS A CHEETAH

Heaps of Hints

❶
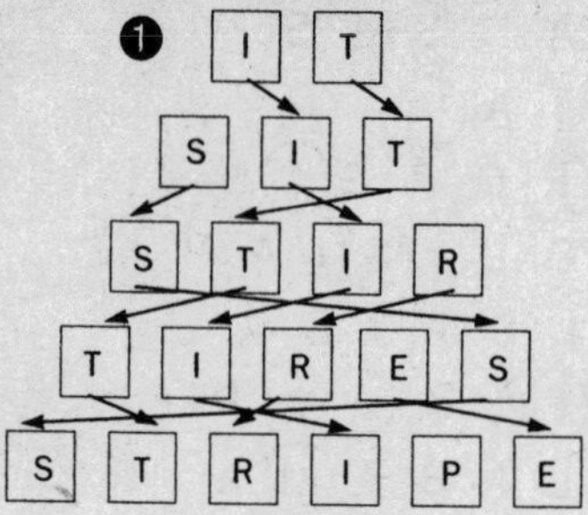

❷
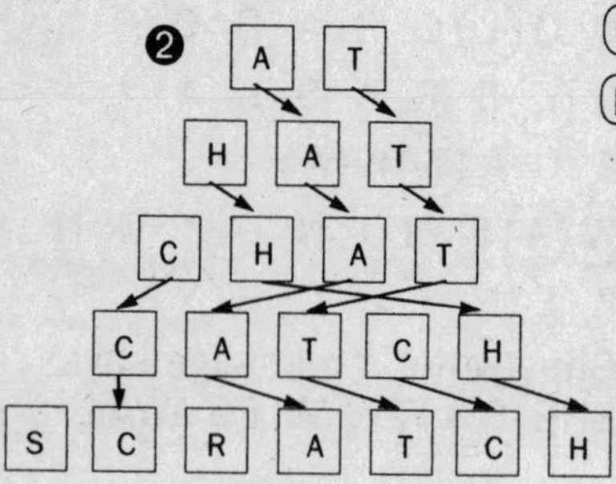

Inside Track

T	M	S	T	O	R	M	U	D	R	R	D
O	D	L	O	C	D	Y	N	E	F	A	S
R	E	M	M	U	S	I	T	D	R	I	U
N	W	O	N	S	W	N	U	F	O	N	N
A	M	O	O	N	I	O	O	O	S	T	W
D	P	R	I	W	L	L	A	F	T	F	A
O	E	N	A	C	I	R	R	U	H	O	R
L	I	G	H	T	N	I	N	G	N	G	M
R	E	D	N	U	H	T	E	C	I	T	S

Clue the Booksnatcher left behind: MUDDY FOOTPRINTS

Shoe Clue

	S	L	A	D	N	A	S	
S	S						L	S
R	L	S	G	O	L	C	E	K
E	I		C		S		E	I
K	P		L	S	K		H	S
A	P		E	P	A		H	T
E	E		A	M	T		G	O
N	R		T	U	E		I	O
S	S		S	P	S		H	B

Tricky Transmission

The secret message says: WHY DID THE SINGER CURL HIMSELF AROUND A PIECE OF GUM? HE WANTED TO BE A RAPPER!

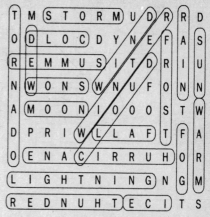

Made It!

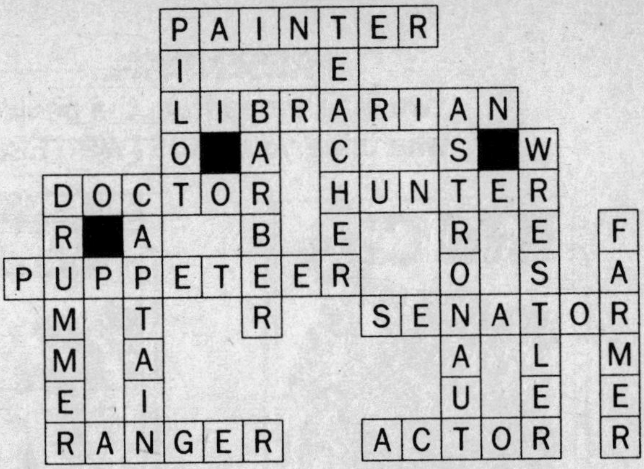

It's a Tough One

End of the Line

1) Forest
2) Little
3) Zebra
4) Study
5) Zip Code
6) Geese
7) Straight
8) Farmer
9) Fever
10) Elephant

The numbered letters spell out: READ THE FIRST LETTER OF EVERY PUZZLE TITLE FOR A SECRET MESSAGE

The Booksnatcher's secret message says: GOODBYE, DETECTIVES. YOU WIN—THIS TIME!

Bonus

Bonus Puzzle: A secret message from Ghostwriter can be found by reading the titles of the books in the Booksnatcher's hand. Find every page where a drawing of the Booksnatcher appears and read the titles of the books in order. The message says: "If you're reading this message, then you're on the team."

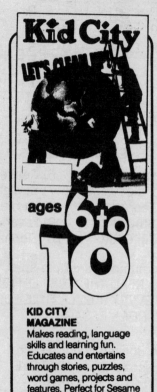

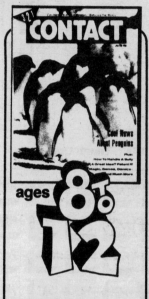